Captain Jack Crawford

Camp Fire Sparks

Captain Jack Crawford

Camp Fire Sparks

ISBN/EAN: 9783337249052

Printed in Europe, USA, Canada, Australia, Japan

Cover: Foto ©Andreas Hilbeck / pixelio.de

More available books at **www.hansebooks.com**

CAMP FIRE SPARKS

BY

CAPTAIN JACK CRAWFORD

"THE POET SCOUT"

When 'round the camp fire comrades sit,
  In open air or hall or tent,
The chambers of each heart are lit
  With sparks of fun and sentiment.

CHICAGO
CHARLES H. KERR AND COMPANY
1893

CONTENTS.

A WORD AT THE START.

——o——

For several years, often without the least provocation, I have been in the habit of reciting my army poems and singing my army songs whenever I could corral a squad of my old comrades yet possessing vitality enough to survive the affliction. So far I have escaped with my life, and with but few bruises, for which I am truly grateful to the kind providence which has stood by me.

Often after reciting some of the crude offspring of my somewhat erratic brain, I have been besieged by comrades who desired to secure copies of them, and on innumerable occasions I have been urged to group them together in a little book, so that all might secure them. Yielding to these many importunities, I have selected a few that I regard as the best of my soldier poems and songs, and I now send them forth under the title "Camp Fire Sparks."

With the earnest wish that their perusal may in a small measure light the path of many an old veteran who is nearing the picket lines of the eternal camp above, I am, comrades,   Yours in F. C. and L.

J. W. CRAWFORD,

"CAPTAIN JACK."

CAMP FIRE SPARKS.

OLD ABNER BROWN.

(Dedicated to the Gallant Volunteer Soldiers of Indiana.)

Not far from a quiet rural town,
In Indiana, dwelt Abner Brown.
Full six foot three in his home-knit socks,
He could strike a blow that would fell an ox.
His time-touched hair stood erect, and seemed,
As an iron-gray crown over eyes which gleamed,
When fired with rage, or alight with mirth,
As the coals in the fireplace over his hearth.

Two idols only old Abner had,
A good old wife and an honest lad,
A sturdy youth, who, the neighbors said,
From his cowhide boots to his shaggy head,
In voice and action and restless fire,
Was an artist's proof of his aged sire.
And the old man's love was lavished upon
The faithful mother and rugged son.

Their home was a house of rough-hewn logs,
They kept their horses and cows and hogs,
And toiled on the farm day after day,
In a sort of automatic way.
Till they grew to care but a trifle what
Transpired away from that rural spot,

Yet read they carefully o'er and o'er
The news which the County papers bore.

Old Abner boasted of fighting stock,
And to patient listeners long would talk,
Of his father's deeds in the many frays
Which tinctured the old Colonial days,
And then, as a sequel, would tell how he,
Imbued with his old sire's loyalty,
On many a bloody field had fought,
'Neath Mexico's sun with Taylor and Scott.

One day when the weekly press-damp sheet,
Was thrown from the stage at old Abner's feet,
The driver cried: "There is Hell to pay!
Old Abe wants volunteers right away!"
He grasped the paper with eager hand,
And paled as its pages his keen eyes scanned,
For the angry bellow of Sumpter's gun,
Had told to the world that the war was on.

He set his teeth as in lock of death,
And curses rode on his heated breath,
For the hands of traitors had dared to fire
On the flag 'neath which had battled his sire.
His boy, just verging on manhood's dawn,
With the old man's valor and nerve and brawn,
In open-lipped wonder stood and heard
The startling dispatches word for word.

"May the God of Heaven," the old man cried,
"In His power sweep the threatened storm aside,
And unnerve the arms that would dare assail
The flag of our country with leaden hail!
May the fury of heaven envelope those,
Who have from their loyalty turned to foes—

Who have leveled with traitorous hands the gun
At the flag of my father and Washington.

"I followed Taylor that bloody day,
When our flag was planted at Monterey,
And held my place in the fierce attack,
Which humbled our foes at Chepultepec,
And now when my country calls once more,
For help for the flag our fathers bore,
My blood runs riot in every vein,
And I'll bare my breast to the storm again!"

With pallid lips his old wife replied:
"Nay, Abner, you must not leave my side.
The flash in the eyes of our brave boy there,
The tint of the coming battles' glare,
Tells all too plainly that *he* will go,
And meet on the field our country's foe.
Our Zack will bring not the coward's shame
On yours and your father's war-honored name.

"But one can I spare" said the loyal wife,
"For I'm drawing near to the eve of life,
And one of my loves must stay at my side,
Till I feel the chill of death's rolling tide.
Zack, my brave boy, since our country's birth,
The Browns in battle have proved their worth,
And the day now dawns when that loyal name
Demands from you a new crown of fame."

The youth's cheeks reddened with patriot fire,
As he knelt at the feet of his gray-haired sire.
His life to his country pledged he there,
For the life of the Union he'd do and dare.
Warm was the blessing the old man gave,
Warm was the kiss from the mother brave,

And sleep came not to their eyes that night,
For Zack would start at the morning light.

Drawn up at the depot the volunteers,
'Mid goodbyes and blessings, and whispered fears,
Awaited the train which should bear them down,
To the terrible shadow of war's dark frown.
There were sobs and wailings, and tearful prayers,
As the stirring drums beat the martial airs,
And the founts of grief to their depths were stirred
When the roar of the coming train was heard.

Old Abner stood like a monarch grand,
And took his son by the toil-scarred hand:
"My son do yer duty whar'ever you go,
Keep yer honest face ever toward the foe.
Guard well the honor of that good name,
Which yer sire and yer grandsire clothed with fame.
Goodbye, my loyal, beloved son—
Write an' let's know how yer comin' on."

Fiercer and fiercer the conflict raged,
And Abner chafed like a lion caged,
And murmured loud at the ties which bound
Him far away from the battle ground.
The fires of valor within his breast,
Caused his heart to throb with a wild unrest,
As the parson read to the eager groups,
The deeds of the Indiana troops.

Heavy as lead seemed his great hand when
O'er the sheet he would guide the old quill pen,
Tracing the news of the home to Zack,
Of the corn in tassel, the wheat in stack
How his mother feebler and feebler grew,

How the news of their battles like wildfire flew,
And he'd close; "Write quick as you kin, my son,
An' let us know how yer comin' on."

O'er a new-made grave stood old Abner Brown,
At the fresh-laid sod gazing sadly down.
His face was drawn with the cords of pain,
As he said in a low and faltering strain:
"Goodbye, old wife—you are safe at rest,
Your loyal soul is among the blest;
While here in repose you peacefully lie,
I go to the battle, Goodbye, Goodbye."

Young Brown on guard near the sleeping camp,
Heard off in the distance a measured tramp,
And through the shadows a form drew nigh,
Like a giant outlined against the sky.
"Halt! Who comes there!" With a movement quick,
His musket hammer was heard "Click-Click!"
When a voice came forth from the hazy dawn,
"Hullo thar, Zack, how you comin' on?"

Together amid the hot battle-fire,
Shoulder to shoulder fought son and sire,
And the records in yon State House to-day,
Recount their gallantry in the fray.
And right in the cauldron of fiery hell
A fragment hurled from exploding shell,
With the shriek of a demon struck young Brown's head,
And he sank 'mid the dying and the dead.

Sank as the Southron hosts drew near,
With the rebel yell and the victor's cheer,
And the ranks of the Union were driven back,
And Abner was swept from the form of Zack.

Not long did the Hoosier boys give way,
To the charging foe on that dreadful day,
But the tide of battle they backward tossed,
And quickly regained the ground they'd lost.

When the day was won and the foe crushed back,
Old Abner sought o'er the field for Zack,
Forms turned he over with trembling hand,
And death-paled features he eager scanned.
A thousand faces his torch revealed,
As he sought through the night on that bloody field,
But the one which he feared might meet his gaze,
Was missing from out of that pallid maze.

Through the years of the war old Abner fought,
And great the slaughter his strong arm wrought;
And God in mercy hid from his ken,
The horrors of Belle Isle's prison pen,
Hid from his ken his demented son,
A pale, wan skeleton, living on,
When all of the world was dead unto
The brain which the shell-wound overthrew.

For years and years on his search intent,
To our great reunions old Abner went,
Seeking the son whom the cruel fates
Had buried beneath an asylum's gates.
In unbelief he would shake his head,
When comrades assured him his boy was dead,
And oft from his breast was the query drawn:
"I wonder how Zack is a comin' on."

Had he known what surgical skill had wrought,
Had he known how oft to the old home spot,

The home he'd abandoned long years before,
His Zack, with heart all heavy and sore,
Had sought for his sire by a hope-spark led,
Had been told, oh, so often, he must be dead,
The happy reunion for which he prayed,
Would not for the long years have been delayed.

One year ago when the veteran throng,
With joy and laughter and story and song,
In response to the annual bugle call,
Were massed at the nation's Capital,
A bent old soldier with snow-white hair,
His face all seamed with the lines of care,
Went tottering up through the busy street,
Half lifting half dragging his weary feet.

Eager the look on the wearied face,
As onward he moved with unsteady pace,
His palsied head keeping time to the beat,
Of the rattling drums in the blue-thronged street.
Eager the glances the old eyes threw
Into the faces of boys in blue,
Who hither and thither moved restlessly,
Like the murmuring waves of a rolling sea.

The spark of hope in his breast sank low,
Till he scarce could feel its encouraging glow,
As he noted each passing face was not
The face of the lost one for whom he sought.
Yet onward and onward and onward he went,
Till he stood at the door of a wide-spread tent,
Where the hours of the evening were sped along,
With speech and story and war-time song.

A voice from the song-group caught his ear,

And with expectation near drowned with fear,
He pushed his way through the merry throng,
To the fountain head of the stirring song.
With wild glad hope did his breast expand,
As, shading his eyes with his palsied hand,
He gazed on the comrades who sang in glee,
Of the days when Sherman marched to the sea.

His face grew pale as the face of death,
And faster and faster came his breath,
As the face of a brawny boy in blue,
Imprinted its lines on his aged view..
Then teardrops coursed from his dimning eyes,
As he tottered forward in glad surprise,
And cried through a smile bright as heaven's dawn,
"Hello! thar, Zack! how you comin' on!"

"WEEDS OF THE ARMY."

Some of the papers tell us that the boys of the G. A. R.
Never smelt smoke in battle, nor went to the front in war—
They brazenly tell us our roster bears only the names of
  those
Who paused at the roar of conflict and northward pointed
  their toes.
They say that the true, brave soldiers have never entered
  our ranks,
That we never were known to muster but a lot of political
  cranks—
As one of the papers put it, we are but the weeds of the
  crop—
But loafers and shirks and cowards, who never heard mus-
  kets pop.

Who are these traitorous writers who are casting their venomous slime
O'er men who gave all to their country at that trying, terrible time?
They are the cringing cowards who never dared go to the
  front,
And stand with our fearless soldiers and help bear the battle's brunt.
They clung to the skirts of women, and soon as our backs
  were turned,
Our flag, our cause and our country the cowardly mis-
  creants spurned.

Go seek them wherever they loiter, from the gulf to the
   northern lakes,
And you'll find them but treacherous, venomous, hideous
   copperhead snakes.

Let us pause on a shaded corner and see a procession pass
At a great Grand Army reunion, when the veterans form in
   mass,
Just note the dismembered bodies, the crutches and canes
   and scars,
That mutely tell us the story of the bloodiest of wars.
Just gaze on the flags they are bearing, all riddled with
   shot and shell,
The flags they carried undaunted right into the gateway of
   hell—
See the bodies bent and disabled, made so in the battles'
   fierce blast;
Are these the weeds of the army at whom these insults are
   cast?

Brave Garfield, our honored martyr, wore the badge of the
   boys in blue.
And Hancock, the mighty soldier, was a comrade tried and
   true,
And Logan, our own loved Logan, undaunted in peace and
   war,
Was proud to be called a member in the ranks of the G. A. R.
And Grant, the intrepid chieftain, who was honored in every
   land,
Stood in the ranks of veterans, a comrade noble and grand,
And Sherman, our "Uncle Billy," God bless his old grizzled
   head,
Rejoiced in being a comrade of the boys he so valiantly led.

Go search o'er the peopled country for the heroes who
    fought in the war,
And you'll find on each notable bosom the eagle and flag
    and star—
'Tis worn as a badge of honor o'er hearts that were loyal
    and true,
And is borne by the greatest soldiers who ever the bright
    sword drew.
Glance over the mighty roster, and pause at each honored
    name,
And reflect for a passing moment o'er each hero's deathless
    fame,
Then answer me this one question, if you find it is in your
    power:
If these are the weeds of the army, in God's name where is
    the flower?

THAR' WAS JIM.

Wildest boy in all the village,
   Up to every wicked lark,
Happy at a chance to pillage
   Melon patches in the dark.
Seemed a 'tarnal mischief breeder,
   Fur in every wicked whim,
Put your hand upon the leader,
   Thar' was Jim.

He war eighteen when the summons
   Come fur Union volunteers,
An' the fifin's an' the drummin's
   An' the patriotic cheers,
Made us with excitement dance, sir,
   Even old men, staid an' prim,
An' among the fust to answer,
   Thar' was Jim.

One day when Gin'ral wanted
   Volunteers to charge a place
Whar' the rebel banners flaunted
   Imperdently in our face,
Seemed as though the cannons' bellers
   Had no skeerishness fur him,
Fur among the foremost fellers,
   Thar' was Jim.

18

How we cheered 'em at the startin'
  On that fearful charge they made,
Fur it seemed that death was sartin
  In that fiery ambuscade.
Once the smoke riz up a showin'
  Them as up the hill they clim,
An' ahead, an' still a goin',
    Thar' was Jim.

Git thar'? Wal, yer jest a screamin',
  Nothin' could have stopped them men—
Each one seemed a howlin' demon
  Chargin' on a fiery pen.
Purty tough w'en next I found him,
  Fur with face all black an' grim,
Dead, with dead men all around him,
    Thar' was Jim.

Friend o' mine? I reckon, sorter—
  Met him fust one winter night—
Lord! but wa'n't that storm a snorter
  W'en I went fur Doctor White!
W'en I heerd my wife a pleadin'
  Me to come an' look at him,
Lyin' in her arms a feedin',
    Thar' was Jim.

A HAPPY HIT.

Everybody shuck their heads,
  In a doobious sort o' way;
Talked about folks makin' beds,
  Inter which they'd have to lay,
All because young Marcus Pike
  Sort of sidled up to me,
An' because I acted like
  I war' summat fond o' he.

Sister Marthy raved an' tore,
  Said I would disgrace our name,
Brother William ripped an' swore,
  Father acted fur from tame.
Mother didn't seem to keer,
  Fur she acted quiet like,
Jes' as if she had no fear
  That I'd marry Marcus Pike.

Marthy had a strappin' beau
  Clerkin' in Si Allen' store,
Six foot tall, an' seemed to know
  Everything; the clothes he wore
War' the best Si Allen kep'
  In his place, an' Marthy thought
That his milingtary step
  Marked the hero to a dot.

Marthy war' the oldest, an'
  Tol' me I had much to learn,
An' I'd better hol' my han'
  Till I got a beau like her'n.
But their oppersition jest
  Seemed to make me like him more.
An' I done my level best,
  His affection to secure.

When the bloody war bruk out,
  Mark jes' couldn't stay to hum,
An' I heerd 'im whoop an' shout,
  Follerin' the fife an' drum.
When he come to say goodbye,
  I kep' vowin' through my tears,
I'd have none but him ef I
  Had to wait a million years.

Marthy's feller said he guessed
  War 'd not agree with him—
That the fire 'at moved the rest,
  War' a sort o' sudden whim.
So right in the store he stuck,
 · Spite o' w'at the neighbors said,
That he didn't have the pluck
  Fur to face the rebel lead.

Well, all through them bloody years,
  I war' true as death to Mark,
An' I calkilate my tears
  Would 'a floated Noah's ark.
Marthy's feller married her.
  An' she allus kep' a sayin'

I war' jest a donkey fur
   All my waitin' and my prayin'.

But at last the fight war' o'er.
   An' amid the people's cheers,
An' a anvil's deaf'nin' roar,
   An' us wimmen's joyful tears,
Back come Marcus an' the rest,
   An', not carin' who war' seein',
i jes' hugged 'im to my breast,
   Prouder than a royal queen.

How the years have seemed to fly,
   Since I wed my soger boy,
He seems proud o' me, an' I
   Seem to swim in ceaseless joy,
An' I reckon Marthy sees
   That I made a happy hit—
Mark is jestis o' the peace—
   Her ol' man's aclerkin' yit.

THE VETERAN AND HIS GRANDSON.

Hold on! Hold on! My goodness, you take my breath, my
    son,
A firin' questions at me, like shots from a Gatlin' gun—
Why do I wear this eagle an' flag an' brazen star,
An' why do my old eyes glisten when somebody mentions
    war?
And why do I call men "comrade," an' why do my eyes
    grow bright,
When you hear me tell your grandma I'm goin' to post to-
    night?
Come here, you inquisitive rascal, an' set on your granddad's
    knee.
An' I'll try an' answer the broadsides you've been a-firin' at
    me.

Away back thar' in the sixties, and long afore you were
    born,
The news come a-flashin' to us, one bright an' sunny morn,
That some of our Southern brothers, a-thinkin' no doubt
    'twar right,
Had trailed their guns on our banner, an' opened a nasty
    fight.
The great big guns war a-boomin', an' the shot flyin' thick
    an' fast,
An' troops all over the southland war rapidly bein' massed,
An' a thrill went through the nation, a fear that our glo-
    rious land

Might be split an' divided an' ruined by mistaken brothers'
    hand.

Lord! but wa'n't there excitement, an' didn't the boys' eyes
    flash?
An' didn't we curse our brothers fur bein' so foolish an'
    rash?
An' didn't we raise the neighbors with loud an' continued
    cheers,
When Abe sent out a dockyment a-callin' fur volunteers?
An, didn't we flock to the colors when the drums began to
    beat,
An' didn't we march with proud step along this village
    street?
An' didn't the people cheer us when we got aboard the cars,
With the flag a-wavin' o'er us, and went away to the wars?

I'll never forgit your grandma as she stood outside o' the
    train,
Her face as white as a snowdrift, her tears a-fallin' like rain—
She stood thar' quiet an' deathlike, 'mid all o' the rush an'
    noise,
For the war war a-takin' from her her husband an' three
    brave boys—
Bill, Charley, and little Tommy—just turned eighteen, but as
    true
An' gallant a little soldier as ever wore the blue.
It seeméd almost like murder for to tear her poor heart so,
But your granddad *couldn't* stay, baby, an' the boys war de-
    termined to go.

The evenin' afore we started she called the boys to her side,
An' told 'em as how they war always their mother's joy an'
    pride,

An' though her soul was in torture, an' her poor heart bleed-
    in' an' sore,
An' though she needed her darlings, their country needed
    'em more.
She told 'em to do their duty whar'ever their feet might
    roam,
An' to never forgit in battle their mother war prayin' at
    home,
An if (an' the tears nigh choked her) they should fall in
    front o' the foe,
She'd go to her blessed Savior an' ax Him to lighten the
    blow.

Bill lays an' awaits the summons 'neath Spottsylvania's
    sod,
An' on the field of Antietam Charley's spirit went back to
    God;
An' Tommy, our baby Tommy, we buried one starlit night
Along with his fallen comrades, just after the Wilderness
    fight.
The lightnin' struck our family tree, an' stripped it of every
    limb,
A-leavin' only this bare old trunk, a-standin' alone an' grim,
My boy, that's why your grandma, when you kneel to the
    God you love,
Makes you ax Him to watch your uncles, an' make 'em
    happy above.

That's why you sometimes see her with tear-drops in her
    eyes;
That's why you sometimes catch her a-tryin' to hide her
    sighs;
That's why at our great reunions she looks so solemn an'
    sad;

That's why her heart seems a-breakin' when the boys are so
    jolly an' glad;
That's why you sometimes find her in the bedroom overhead,
Down on her knees a-prayin', with their pictures laid out on
    the bed;
That's why the old-time brightness will light up her face no
    more,
Till she meets her hero warriors in the camp on the other
    shore.

An' when the great war was over, back came the veterans
    true,
With not one star a-missin' from that azure field of blue,
An' the boys who on field o' battle had stood the fiery test
Formed posts o' the great Grand Army in the North, South,
    East, an' West.
Fraternity, Charity, Loyalty, is the motto 'neath which
    they train,
Their object to care for the helpless, an' banish sorrow an'
    pain
From the homes o' the widows, an' orphans o', the boys
    who have gone before,
To answer their names at roll-call in that great Grand
    Army Corps.

An' that's why we wear these badges, the eagle an' flag an'
    star.
Worn only by veteran heroes who fought in that bloody
    war;
An' that's why my old eyes glisten when talkin' about the
    fray,
An' that's why I call men "comrade" when I meet 'em
    every day;
An' that's why I tell your grandma, "I'm goin' to post to-
    night."

For thar's where I meet the old boys who stood with me
    in the fight,
And, my child, that's why I've taught you to love and re-
    vere the men
Who come here a-wearin' badges to fight those battles again.

They are the gallant heroes who stood 'mid the shot and
    shell,
An' follered the flyin' colors right into the mouth o' hell—
They are the men whose valor saved the land from disgrace
    an' shame,
An' lifted her back in triumph to her perch on the dome o'
    fame;
An' as long as you live, my darling, till your pale lips in
    death are mute,
When you see that badge on a bosom, take off your hat
    an' salute;
An' if any ol' vet should halt you, an' question why you do,
Just tell him you've got a right to, fur your granddad's a
    comrade too.

An' so you've bin to Washington to that big 'campment
    thar'?
An' since the hoodoo's over I suppose you want to sw'ar
Fur bein' sich a cussed fool a-wastin' of yer cash
To whoop an' yell, an' wa'r a badge, an' all sich useless
    trash.
It seems to me a man's an ass to squander sich a sum
To hear agin the squeakin' fife an' 'tarnal rattlin' drum,
An' see a big, hot, dusty crowd o' fellers sich as us,
An' specchify, an' sing ol' songs, an' make a howlin' fuss.

They've bin a holdin' 'campments now fur—well, fur since
    the war,
An' I ain't bin to ary one, an' wa't is more I sw'ar
That they kin' keep on holdin' 'em till Gabriel's bugle blows,
But 'mong the foolish fellers thar' you wont see Uncle Mose.
I work an' toil mos' 'tarnal hard for all the cash I git,
An' I ain't idiot enough to go an' squander it
Fur these confounded yearly sprees o' men that wore the
    blue—
To put it plainly, Dan, I ain't as big a fool as you.

Bill Thompson thar' an' sent his love? Big S'argent Bill?
    O, no—
I got it purty straight he died a dozen years ago—
Thar' sure enough? Stop lyin', Dan, or you may feel this
    boot,

I swar to gosh I'd give a cow to see that ol' galoot.
How did he look? The durned ol' cuss! Gray as a rat, I
    guess,
Big S'argent Bill, the jolliest boy we had in all our mess,
His heart in keepin' with his bulk, a brave ol' soldier, too—
An' so you seed 'im? Wish to gosh I could a bin with you.

Who? O, shet up! Jack Allison? You didn't see ol' Jack?
If you don't stop yer lyin' Dan, I'll break yer cussed back!
God bless his ol' good natured soul! Say does he mind it
    much
A swoppin' off one o' his legs at Vicksburg for a crutch?·
Poor Jack! That was a fearful shot! A piece of screamin'
    shell
Come shriekin' like a demon from that blazin' line o' hell,
An' left the poor boy layin'. thar' with one leg shattered
    bad,
An' swearin' like a trooper, too! Great guns, but wa'nt he
    mad!

You seed ol' Chaplain Stewart, too? An' Captain Double-
    day?
Say, Dan, I honest don't believe a 'tarnal word you say!
Who? Go to grass! `Not little Tom! the same cute rascal
    still?
By Jinks, I'd ruther see that boy than find a dollar bill.
An' Simon Gregg? An' Mexico? An' lengthy Oscar Plumb,
Who used to sing the song about that gal he left to hum?
An' Frank Moran, the heartless cuss as stole the Colonel's
    ham.
An' swore it war a colored contraband? *Well-I-be-dam!*

Ed Bassett thar'? I've got you, Dan! That sort o' lie don't
    go,
Fur Ed's a cattle ranchin' now down in New Mexico—

Come all the way to see the boys? Wal, bless his lovin,
    eyes—
That's Ed, though—tackle anything, no matter what the
    size!
Who? Aleck Pierce, as toted me a mile or more one night
When I was wounded in the hip at that durned Shiloh
    fight?
An' *he* was thar; an' said he come a-purpose to see me?
Wal, by the Gods of War! *Say, Dan, Whar'll the next 'un be?*

THE LAST ROLL-CALL.

With pallid face a soldier brave lay dying,
    His life-blood dampening the Southern sod,
While all around him bleeding forms were lying,
    With dim and death touched eyes upturned to God.
On every side the battle roared and thundered,
    And shot and shell with maddening shrieks flew by,
And many souls, from mangled bodies sundered,
    Soared upward to the Master's camp on high.

"Here! Here!" the dying soldier eager muttered,
    And passing comrade knelt above his form
And asked him what he wished—if he had uttered
    The call for help amid the battle's storm?
"Ah!" he replied, "I need no help from mortal,
    (And o'er his face a smile angelic came),
The roll is being called at heaven's portal,
    And I but answered when I heard my name."

JIM'S LETTER.

I sat on the crest of a mountain high
  Overlooking Jornado's plain,
The mocking-bird sang in the woods close by
  In a glad and sweet refrain,
And the doves were cooing among the trees,
  And the deer browsed at my feet,
With the scent of wild flowers perfuming the breeze
  It was Nature in Nature's retreat.

And my heart just danced to the song-bird's tune,
  And forgotten was every care,
And it seemed that balmy and flowery June
  Instead of the Winter was there,
And I rolled in the grass and laughed and sang
  In a joyous and glad refrain,
Till the deer ran off and the old woods rang,
  And the echo came back again.

Then a shot rang out and a bang! bang! bang!
  And my heart leaped again with joy,
And I laughed once more till the old woods rang,
  For I knew it was Harry, my boy.
Then near to my side on his foaming mare
  He stopped, and I held my breath.
His face was the picture of cold despair,
  And as white as the face of death.

"Speak out! Great God, don't look like that,
  With your white face dusty and grim."

Then he said, as he raised his broad-brimmed hat,
  "Here's a letter from Corporal Jim."
And he stole away to a tree close by,
  With his head drooping low on his breast;
I knew it was death by the tear in his eye—
  Jim's letter must tell the rest.

The blood in my veins seemed its course to retrace,
  And the song birds of Heaven were still,
An eclipse came over the sunny face
  Of that joyous and gladsome hill.
All Nature seemed hushed as I held in my hand
  That message from comrade of mine,
And I can't explain and I don't understand,
  But somehow—it started the brine.

With eager eyes and with trembling hand
  I gazed for an instant, and then
My heart stood still; the writing I scanned
  Was from one of God's own noble men.
The seal was broken, and the mist arose
  In my eyes while I read it out:
"Who'll champion us now, God only knows,
  Since Logan is mustered out."

Oh, comrades of mine, he was dearer to me
  Than the wealth of my western wild,
And the soft balmy breeze and the doves on the tree
  Seemed to moan, while I wept like a child.
Yes, boys, and I want you to understand
  What I say I will never take back,
And I thought it was noble and brave and grand
  To cry for a hero like Jack,

To cry in the wildwood when no one was near,
  Save my boy, and he joined me, you bet,

For the child of a soldier to Jack was most dear,
  And his grave with their tears will keep wet.
And who, if not I, should inscribe to the name
  Of that hero now gone to his rest,
A song from the wildwood, the mountain and plain,
  For Black Jack was a son of the West.

Our Great Alexander, our mightiest Chief,
  Every heart-throb that beat in his breast,
Was the music that chimed in his heart for relief
  For our widows and orphans distressed.
--Sincere in his friendship, from trickery free,
  With honesty's stamp on his face,
And we ask, as we bow low to Heaven's decree,
  "Lord, raise up a man in his place."

A man whom the comrades can love and revere,
  A soldier and statesman combined,
Upright in deportment, unconscious of fear,
  Yet modest and gentle and kind.
A man who stood with us on many a field,
  When the shots wildly shrieked in the air,
A man whose convictions never would yield,
  A duplicate Jack, as it were.

Hold 'im? No. A yoke o' steers
  Couldn't held that boy o' mine,
W'en the call fur volunteers
  Come a ringin' down the line.
Patriotism strong an' pure
  Hit 'im like a burstin' bomb—
Sed he'd be a gin'ral. sure,
  W'en he come home.

Course his mother up an' cried,
  Jes' as any mother would
Ef her only joy an' pride
  Went away, perhaps fur good,
But he knocked her reasonin'
  Inter sort o' honey-comb—
Sed he'd make 'er smile ag'in,
  W'en he come home.

Off he marched, an' I suppose
  No one in the regiment
Looked so fine in soger clothes
  As our Bill the day he went.
Neighbors 'lowed he'd turn out bad,
  But we told 'm how we'd show'm
W'at a noble boy we had,
  W'en Bill come home.

34

Got a letter now an' then
  Tellin' how he got along,
How he thought o' mother w'en
  Tempted fur to do a wrong.
"An'," sed he, "you'll shout so loud
  That you'll shatter heaven's dome.
'Cause you'll feel so monst'ous proud
  W'en Bill comes home.

'Mong his letters thar' was one
  More'n all the rest, perhaps,
Pleased us, fur he said he'd won
  A leftenant's shoulder straps
Fur his brav'ry in a row
  Down in Georgy, front o' Rome—
Said we'd hold our heads up now
  W'en Bill come home.

Purty soon the papers said,
  That fur conduct o' some sort,
Owin' to the way he led
  Of his sogers 'gin a fort,
Some affair was read out loud
  Makin' of him "Captain" Bloom—
"Lor!" we said, "won't we be proud,
  W'en Bill comes home."

Then the news went o'er the land
  O' that great Atlanter fight,
An' we couldn't understand
  W'y our William didn't write.
Neighbors tried ter lift us out
  O' the orful cloud o' gloom—
Sed they'd come an' help us shout,

W'en Bill come home.

*   *   *   *   *   *

Coffin in the baggage car,
　Black as ever black could be.
All the neighbors standin' thar'
　Pityin' of wife an' me
Meetin' of our darlin' boy
　Jes' ter put 'im in the tomb,
Give us sorrow 'stead o' joy,
　W'en Bill come home.

THE TRUE STORY OF MARCHING THROUGH GEORGIA.

Now lay the good old bugle down and let me toot my horn,
And lay aside the good old song, that's getting somewhat
     worn;
The shoe I think will fit you if you'll all own up the corn,
     As we went marching through Georgia.

We never found a chicken that could roost out of our reach,
We seldom had a chaplain that could find the time to preach,
We never saw a soldier pass a shirt hung out to bleach,
     As we went marching through Georgia.

Oh, how we used to toil along right through the swamps
     and bogs,
And how the ladies blushed at our dilapidated togs,
And how we showed our bravery assassinating hogs,
     As we went marching through Georgia.

When charging on a chicken roost, the rebel girls cried
     "shame!"
And said our actions would disgrace the soldiers' honored
     name.
They came at us with clubs and dogs, but we got there just
     the same,
     As we went marching through Georgia.

When coming in from foraging sometimes we would get
     caught,

The colonel then would paw the ground, and swear he'd
    have us shot,
And then he'd eye our captured fowls and fine us half we
    got,
        As we went marching through Georgia.

Whene'er we'd catch a grandpa goose, too old and tough
    and strong,
And thought it was too rich for us, but good for the "bong
    tong,"
We'd send it to the general, and laugh both loud and long,
        As we went marching through Georgia.

When ordered up some earthwork, or some battery to take,
I've seen some heavy charges, that caused the earth to
    quake,
They were nothing to the charges the sutlers used to make,
        As we were marching through Georgia.

SCENE IN A SOLDIERS' HOME.

Adjutant, read that letter ag'in.
  I kin scarcely believe my ears—
My hearin' is gettin' meaner 'n sin,
  As I creep along in years,
An' it sounds blame funny fur John to say,
He wants me at home ag'in right away.

That's w'at it says, dead sartin, sure,
  An' he calls me his "father dear,"
That—arter drivin' me from his door,
  An' a forcin' of me here.
I reckon the Lord has tuk my part,
By givin' the boy a change o' heart.

An' his wife, she writes a line or two,
  Sayin' how they miss me there,
An' how she weeps at the sad, sad view
  O' my empty easy-chair.
Well, well, w'ats the world a-driving at,
W'en it brings about sich changes as that?

I'll tell you, Adjutant, how it was:
  John married two years ago,
An' said it was fur my good, because
  I was gittin' old, you know,
An' he reckoned we needed a woman there
To 'tend the house and give me some care.

39

She seemed like an angel sproutin' wings,
  Under John's trainin', I guess,
An' she humped around an' looked arter things,
  With remarkable quickliness;
An' to me she was just as good an' kind
As any man's darter you could find.

W'en John came in from the field one day
  He sez to me, "Father," sez he,
"You're a-gittin' old, an' in feeblish way,
  W'y not deed the farm to me?
Then you'll have no care, an' me 'n my wife
Will see to your comfort all your life."

Well, Adjutant, that looked proper, quite,
  An' I told him I was agreed,
An' he went to town to a lawyer that night,
  An' had him make out the deed.
An' then I lolled back in my old arm-chair,
An' thanked the Lord that I hadn't a care.

All at once Amandy got awful cross,
  An' never give me a smile,
An' John begun to tear 'round an' boss
  In a most presumptuous style,
An' if I'd attempt fur to interfere,
He'd crush me by sayin', "I'm master here."

Things kep' a gittin' wuss an' wuss,
  An' it come in my head one day,
Like a shot from an ol'-time blunderbuss,
  That the ol' man was in the way,
An' now that they had the property,
The nex' move was how to get rid of me.

An' so they made a hell on earth
  O' the home I loved so dear,
An' the boy I'd doted upon since his birth
  Insisted on sendin' me here,
An' Amandy chipped in, sayin' spitefully,
'Twas the only place fit for such as me.

An' now they are sorry. Say, Adjutant,
  Jest write 'em a letter fur me,
How happy they've made me, and how I want
  To return to them instantly;
An' tell 'em I thank the good Lord above
For fillin' their hearts with the ol'-time love.

But hol' on! Aha! I see it now—
  Tear that up, and write 'em that I
Am happy an' satisfied here, an' how
  I'll stay right here till I die—
That two thousand dollars back pension I got
Is the Lord that's a-movin' their hearts. Eh? What?

When we gather around the camp fire
　　To talk of battles fought,
Of the camps, the sieges and marches,
　　And our Union so dearly bought,
Let us not forget our comrades,
　　Who their warmest life-blood shed—
When we sound a cheer for the living,
　　Let us drop a tear for the dead.

When the post room rings with laughter,
　　Or resounds with the rattling song,
And we feel so gay and jolly,
　　As the moments speed along,
Let us pause in our merry making,
　　And reverent bow each head,
And still our cheers for the living
　　While we drop a tear for the dead.

In the blazing front of battle,
　　Where shot and shell flew fast,
Where the very ground was reeling,
　　Like a tree before the blast,
The boys who have gone before us,
　　Their blood in the great cause shed—
Then while we cheer for the living
　　Let us drop a tear for the dead.

In the bivouac of heaven,
  On the banks of the sparkling stream,
Where the tree of life is waving,
  Their camp fires radiant gleam,
And there they watch for our coming,
  With the spirits' martial tread—
Then while we cheer for the living
  Let us drop a tear for the dead.

SUNSHINE.

I never like to see a man a 'rastlin' with the dumps
'Cause in the game of life he doesn't always catch the trumps,
  But I can always cotton to a free and easy cuss,
  As takes his dose, and thanks the Lord it isn't any wuss.
There ain't no use o' kickin' and swearin' at your luck,
You can't correct the trouble more'n you can drown a duck.
  Remember, when beneath the load your sufferin' head is
    bowed,
  That God 'll sprinkle sunshine in the trail of every cloud.

If you should see a fellow-man with trouble's flag unfurled,
And lookin' like he didn't have a friend in all the world,
  Go up and slap him on the back, and holler " how d' you
    do,"
  And grasp his hand so warm he'll know he has a friend in
    you.
Then ax him what's a hurtin' 'im, and laugh his cares away,
And tell him that the darkest night is just afore the day.
  Don't talk in graveyard palaver, but say it right out loud,
  That God 'll sprinkle sunshine in the trail of every cloud.

This world at best is but a hash of pleasure and of pain,
Some days are bright and sunny, and some all sloshed with
          rain,
     And that's just how it ought to be, for when the clouds
          roll by
     We'll know just how to 'preciate the bright and smilin'
          sky.
So learn to take it as it comes, and don't sweat at the pores
Because the Lord's opinion doesn't coincide with yours,
     But always keep rememberin', when cares your path
          enshroud.
     That God has lots of sunshine to spill behind the cloud.

SLEEP, SOLDIER, SLEEP.

[A Memorial Day Song.]

Sleep, soldier, sleep, thy warfare is o'er,
War's dread alarums shall wake thee no more,
Sleep, calmly sleep, 'neath the flowering sod,
Waiting the reveille sounded from God.
Over thy resting place bright flowers we twine,
Gratitude's emblems on loyalty's shrine,
Fruits of your valor we gratefully reap,
Freedom and liberty—sleep—sleep—sleep.

          Beautiful flowers of Spring,
          Lovingly here we bring,
     Sacred thy memory ever we'll keep,
          Under the grassy sod,
          Waiting the call from God,
     Sweetly and peacefully—sleep—sleep—sleep.

Rest, soldier, rest, thy peace thou hast earned,
On the red fields where the battle fires burned—
Rest, sweetly rest, for aweary wert thou,
Winning the laurels which circled thy brow.
Soon will the trumpeter wake thee again,
Sounding "Assembly" on heaven's bright plain,
There with your comrades in realms of the blest,
Through all eternity, rest, sweet rest.

Beautiful flowers of Spring,
Lovingly here we bring,
Sacred thy memory ever we'll keep,
Under the grassy sod,
Waiting the call from God,
Sweetly and peacefully—sleep—sleep—sleep.

WHO THE HEROES WERE.

You "never was scared in battle?" Here,
   Old comrade, don't make a break like that!
The man don't live who was free from fear
   When the vicious bullets began to spat,
And the cannons belched from their iron throats
   The deafening notes of the song of war—
The frightful, terrible, thundering notes
   That caused the eternal earth to jar.

I've heard men say they were just as cool
   In the heat of battle as they would be
In a quiet seat in a Sabbath school,
   But they couldn't find a believer in me.
I never flinched, never shirked a call,
   But several times in the war swept south
If I'd been shot through the heart the ball
   Would have had to hit me square in the mouth.

It's the silliest sort of talk we hear—
   And hear from soldiers of solid worth—
That they stood in the front and felt no fear
   When the rumblings of battle convulsed the earth.
I hold that our bravest men were those
   Who felt alarm at the cannon's roar,
Yet never rearward pointed their toes,
   But stood like men till the battle was o'er.

NOT A SIN TO LIE THAT WAY.

The old vets now will often sit and tell their loving wives
Of many stirring incidents that crossed their soldier lives—
The marches, camps and sieges, the battles hard they fought,
And how they stood up gallantly amid the storms of shot;
But raids on chicken rendezvous they'll swear they never
     made,
Nor never helped assassinate a hog in Southern glade,
Nor never "beat" the Sutler when they drew their monthly
     pay—
They seem to think it not a sin to lie that way.

They'll talk of great privations they were called on to endure,
And how they'd laugh at hardships which their "kicking"
     couldn't cure—
The beating rains, the driving snows, and many a dire
     distress
They will relate in sentences of glowing vividness.
They'll scowl with indignation at hint of how they shirked,
And how the many "soldier" games successfully they worked;
They never dodged guard duty, but were always prompt,
     they'll say,
And seem to think it not a sin to lie that way.

They'll tell of how from blanket beds their truant thoughts
     would roam
Unto the dear, good, loyal girls they left in distant home,
And how their martial hearts would throb with rapture at
     the thought

47

Of sweethearts' loving welcome when the battles all were
      fought.
Just hint to one that he was sweet on some fair Southern
      girl,
He'll shake his head emphatic and his lip will scornful curl;
He'll say that to his own love he was loyal every day,
And seem to think it not a sin to lie that way.

With faces tinged with sorrow as memory takes them back,
They'll tell of pangs of hunger when the rations would get
      slack,
And how the corn from mules they'd filch, so desp'rate did
      they grow,
While staring in starvation's face in chase of Southern foe.
And then with look of innocence they'll tell of many a raid
Their more ungodly comrades on the big plantations made,
But raiding was a crime which at their own doors didn't
      lay—
They seem to think it not a sin to lie that way.